PUPPY PIRATES

X Marks the Spot

by Erin Soderberg

illustrations by Russ Cox

A STEPPING STONE BOOK™

Random House 🏠 New York

For Michelle Nagler, a treasure
of an editor
—E.S.

Text copyright © 2015 by Erin Soderberg Downing and Robin Wasserman
Cover art copyright © 2015 by Luz Tapia
Interior illustrations copyright © 2015 by Russ Cox

Visit us on the Web! randomhousekids.com
SteppingStonesBooks.com
Educators and librarians, for a variety of teaching tools, visit us at
RHTeachersLibrarians.com

Library of Congress Cataloging-in-Publication Data
Soderberg, Erin.
X marks the spot / Erin Soderberg. — First edition.
pages cm. — (Puppy pirates ; #2)
Summary: "Wally and his human friend Henry have passed the test.
They are now officially Puppy Pirates—and just in time for an exciting
new adventure. A treasure hunt! The puppies sail to a deserted island
with treasure map in paw, and ready to dig. But uh-oh! This island isn't
deserted after all . . ."—Provided by publisher.
ISBN 978-0-553-51170-3 (pbk.) — ISBN 978-0-553-51171-0 (lib. bdg.) —
ISBN 978-0-553-51172-7 (ebook)
[1. Dogs—Fiction. 2. Pirates—Fiction. 3. Buried treasure—Fiction.
4. Adventure and adventurers—Fiction.] l. Title.
PZ7.S685257Xm 2015 [Fic]—dc23 2014039406

Printed in the United States of America
10 9 8 7 6 5 4 3 2 1

This book has been officially leveled by using the F&P Text Level Gradient™
Leveling System.

X Marks the Spot

Ahoy, mateys!

Set sail for adventure with the

PUPPY PIRATES

#1 *Stowaway!*
#2 *X Marks the Spot*

Coming Soon:
#3 *Catnapped!*

CONTENTS

Pug Pranks

Drip.

Drip.

Splat!

Little drops of something wet rained down on Captain Red Beard's desk. The scraggly terrier looked left, then right, then down. He was trying to find the leak in his cabin.

The only place he didn't look? *Up.* So he didn't see the two naughty pugs peering down at him through a hole in his ceiling.

Above the captain, Puggly scolded her sister, "Put your tongue back in your mouth, Piggly! You're droolin' on the captain. If he sees us up here, we're done for!"

Piggly and Puggly loved to make mischief. They also loved to spy. The two pugs had been working on digging open a spy hole above the captain's quarters for months. They had finally broken through. And just in time, too! The puppy pirate captain was having an important meeting with his first mate, Curly. And the pugs planned to hear every word of it.

Wally, a cuddly golden retriever, squeezed in for a closer look. "What if they catch us?" he whispered, peering down at Curly and the captain.

Wally and his best mate, a human boy named Henry, were the newest members of the puppy pirate crew. They had worked hard to convince Captain Red Beard to let them stay on board the ship. Wally didn't want him to change his mind!

"In case you were wondering, it's my turn," Henry said, pressing his face to the hole. "I don't see any maps."

"Shhh," Wally said, nuzzling his wet nose into Henry's shoulder.

Wally and Henry loved everything about being pirates—fighting the enemy kitten ship, joining in on daring adventures, singing pirate songs, and all the great friends they had already made. Wally whispered, "I don't want to get in trouble with Captain."

"Aw, quit your worryin'," said Piggly, her gold tooth glinting. "Do you wanna get the map, or don'tcha?"

Wally did. He had never seen a real treasure map. And this map was drawn by the most famous puppy pirate in history, Growlin' Grace! Many years ago, the fierce pirate captain had buried her pirate booty on an island called the Boneyard. Right after she'd buried her loot, Growlin' Grace had disappeared . . . along with the one and only map to the treasure.

After years of searching, Captain Red Beard had finally gotten his paws on the famous map! So now the puppy pirates were on course for the Boneyard—and the greatest treasure hunt of all time.

Wally and Henry wanted to get a look at the map *before* they landed on the island. And Piggly and Puggly were happy to help. Especially since spying was involved.

Puggly's curly tail wagged. Fancy pink beads swished to and fro, swatting Wally in the face. Puggly loved to get dressed up, even when she was in the middle of making mischief. "Here's the plan, mates," Puggly whispered. "See that metal box on the captain's desk? That's where the treasure map is hidden. Piggly and I have the perfect way to get it."

"Arrrrf!" agreed Piggly. She showed them a horseshoe-shaped magnet hanging from a long cord. "See this? It sticks to metal like glue. We'll have the map in our paws in no time." Piggly gripped the cord between her teeth. Very carefully, she lowered the magnet through the spy

hole. Wally and Henry held their breath.

Down, down, down the magnet went— straight into the captain's quarters. It hung a few feet over the captain's desk.

"Did you hear something?" Captain Red Beard growled, his ears alert.

Wally, Henry, and the pugs froze. The captain and Curly were both sitting on plaid cushions in front of Red Beard's desk. If either of them looked up, they would see the magnet hanging from the cord. And if they followed the cord all the way up to the spy hole, they would spot the spies.

And that would mean *big* trouble.

"I don't hear anything, Captain," Curly yipped. "Let's focus. We have to come up with a plan."

Wally sighed with relief. Quietly.

The magnet dangled over the desk. Piggly

grunted. "Heavy," she growled. She wiggled her chubby body and tried to get a better grip with her teeth. "The magnet . . . it be heavy!" Suddenly, the cord holding the magnet dropped from between her teeth.

Like a snake, the cord wriggled through the spy hole. Henry grabbed for it and caught it just in time. Piggly nosed forward and grabbed for the cord with her teeth again.

But then Captain Red Beard jumped up and grabbed hold of the other end! The captain bit down hard on the cord and tugged.

Piggly didn't want to let her magnet go. It was too useful for pranks. So she tugged harder.

Back and forth the pups tugged. The floorboards underneath the spies creaked and groaned.

"Uh, I don't think that's a good sound," Henry said. "Maybe you should let go."

That's when the captain gave one last, furious yank on the cord. The floorboards moaned louder than ever.

Then they snapped.

Piggly, Puggly, Henry, and Wally all toppled through the hole in the floor and landed in a heap. Right on the captain's desk.

Captain Red Beard growled at the intruders.

"Ahoy," squeaked Wally.

The captain glared. In a scratchy voice he barked, "Avast! What are ya scurvy dogs doin' in me quarters?"

"Spies!" yipped his first mate in her tiny voice. Curly was a puffy white mini poodle who looked as fierce as a piece of lemon meringue pie. But she was the smartest, toughest pup on board. "Someone ought to keep you pugs on a leash. You're nothin' but trouble."

"Sorry, Captain," murmured Puggly. She

smiled under her foofy pink hair bows. "We just wanted a peek at the treasure map."

The captain and Curly looked at each other. Then Red Beard popped open the metal box on his desk. He sighed and laid his head on his paws. "Go ahead and have a look." The group all crowded around the map. "But a look's not gonna be worth much. Because Growlin' Grace's treasure map . . . is blank!"

Magic Map

"Blank?" barked Puggly.

"But—but that's impossible!" yipped Piggly. "How will we find Growlin' Grace's treasure if the map is blank?"

Captain Red Beard scratched behind his ear. "That's what Curly and I were tryin' to figure out." He nosed the map into the middle of his desk. Except for the words GROWLIN' GRACE'S GREATEST TREASURE at the top, the rest of the old yellowed paper was empty.

Wally felt his hopes sink. His first-ever treasure hunt was doomed already.

Henry leaned forward and squinted at the blank piece of parchment. "In case you were wondering, pirates used to draw their maps in invisible ink. Maybe if we hold the map up to something hot, like a candle, the ink will reappear."

The puppy pirates all stared at him. Red Beard was the first to laugh. "Invisible ink? That sounds like hoogly-boogly magic."

"Rubbish," agreed Curly.

Wally took a nervous breath, then said, "Excuse me, Captain? Henry knows everything there is to know about pirates. Maybe we should try it, just to see?"

Captain Red Beard looked uncertain. "What say you, Curly? Do we take advice from little Walty's boy?"

Curly sniffed. "I suppose it can't hurt."

The captain nosed the paper toward the drippy candle on his desk. Forgetting that paper and fire don't go well together, he pushed it a bit too close to the candle. The edge of the paper began to smoke, then burn. Piggly leaped forward and snagged the map, pulling it away from the candle. Puggly stomped on it, just before the whole page would have gone up in flames.

"Uh, Captain, maybe we should let Henry try," Wally said. "Since it was his idea."

The captain grumbled and scowled, but he agreed to let Henry give it a try.

Henry made sure to hold the map a couple of inches *over* the flame, so it couldn't catch fire. As the paper heated up, dark symbols and letters began to appear.

"Shiver me timbers, it's a miracle," said the captain.

Just as the final lines on the map came into view, the whole ship rumbled and shook. It felt like they'd hit something!

"Iceberg!" screamed Captain Red Beard. "Abandon ship!" He dove under the desk and hid his head beneath his paws.

The other dogs looked at him strangely. "Captain?" said Curly. "Sir, we're in the South Seas. There *are* no icebergs."

Red Beard poked his nose out from beneath

the desk. "Of course there are no icebergs. I knew that." Then he yelped in alarm. "Sea monster? I think we're being attacked by the Sea Slug!"

From above decks, someone hollered, "Land ho! The bounty of the Boneyard awaits!"

Captain Red Beard yipped gleefully. "It's just like I said: we're here!" He bounded out of his hiding place. "Yo ho haroo—Boneyard, here we come!"

The captain dashed through the narrow halls and up to the main deck of their ship, the *Salty Bone*. The other puppies raced behind him. In all the excitement, Wally was the only one who remembered Growlin' Grace's map. He nudged it toward Henry, who tucked the map into one of his giant pockets for safekeeping. Then he stuck the pugs' magnet in there, too.

Just in case.

The puppy pirates lowered the long wooden platform that stretched between the huge ship and the sandy island. The crew zoomed across the gangway onto the sand. Everyone was excited about the chance to hunt for treasure. But they were also excited to play in the waves and dig on the beach and romp through the trees. After weeks on a stinky pirate ship, it was time to run free!

As the rest of the puppies played fetch and chased waves, the oldest member of the pirate crew grumped and growled. Old Salt, a peg-legged Bernese mountain dog, had very strong opinions about treasure.

"What's wrong, Old Salt?" asked Wally. He dragged a nice, thick stick over for the old pirate

to chew on. "You don't look excited about our treasure hunt."

"Well, pup, I've always found that treasure hunts are more trouble than they're worth." He chewed the stick thoughtfully.

"What do you mean?" Wally asked.

"Sometimes pups forget to enjoy the treasure they already have," Old Salt said. Wally looked at him curiously, but the old dog would say nothing more.

Wally ran off to play with the pugs and Henry. The pugs had found some hollow bamboo shoots that were fun to blow air through. Soon, Piggly found a bush full of wild blueberries. After she ate her fill, she loaded her bamboo straw with berries and blew them at her friends. Some berries pinged off the dogs' fur, while others splatted on contact.

Henry lay down to rest on the warm beach sand. This gave Piggly and Puggly another excellent idea. They began to dig. In just a few minutes, Henry was totally covered in sand. That looked like fun to Wally, so he lay down next to Henry. The pugs buried him, too.

The four friends were having such a great time that they didn't realize the rest of the crew had gathered on the other end of the beach, by the edge of a dark green jungle. They were about to set off on the treasure hunt . . . without Wally, Henry, and the pugs!

"Wait for us!" Wally yelped, but the others were too far away to hear. He wriggled and squirmed in the sand, but it was no use. He was buried up to his neck.

Piggly and Puggly dug Wally and Henry out of the sand as fast as they could. But their legs were short, and it wasn't fast enough. By the time Wally and Henry were free, the rest of the crew was long gone.

Wally ran to the edge of the trees and sniffed

around for a familiar scent. But there were too many new and exciting smells. He couldn't figure out which ones belonged to his crew— or where they might have gone.

"It looks like we're on our own," said Henry, coming up behind Wally. He reached into his pocket, and Wally heard something crinkle. "But in case you were wondering? I still have the map!"

Treasure Talk

"We still have the map!" Wally cried joyfully. He leaped in the air. He rolled around in the sand. He wagged his tail as hard as he could. Then he realized something, and his tail stopped wagging. "But we're also all alone." He swallowed and pulled his golden velvety ears in close against his head. Wally hated to be alone.

He peered into the jungle. The trees were emerald green and massive. They were even higher than the crow's nest on the *Salty Bone*.

Until then, the ship was the tallest thing Wally had ever seen.

"We're not alone," said Puggly. "We have each other."

"And the map!" Piggly reminded them. "Let's figure out which way we're supposed to go." She snatched the map out of Henry's hand.

"Treasure!" screeched Puggly. Puggly *loved* beautiful things. She couldn't wait to see what jewels and riches Growlin' Grace might have buried. "Treasure, treasure, treasure, treasure—"

Piggly bumped her rump against her sister's to get her to stop yapping. They had work to do. Treasure-tracking work.

Wally unrolled the map and held it open with his two front paws. There were a lot of lines and symbols and squiggly stuff. None of it made sense.

Henry got down on his knees beside Wally.

"Look! Here is where we are—this beach. And there's the X. In case you were wondering, X always marks the treasure spot." He pointed at a big X in the bottom corner of the map.

Wally looked at the map. The path toward the X started at the beach and wove through the jungle. He knew they were running out of time. If they didn't chase after the captain and the others soon, they would be too far behind to ever catch up. And when the captain realized he didn't have the map? He would be furious. Wally did not like when the captain was angry.

"The others went this way," Wally said, nosing into the trees. "We can hunt for the crew and the treasure at the same time."

Because he was the tallest, Henry led. Wally followed, with Piggly and Puggly trotting along at the rear.

Wally was born on a farm and had only heard

about the jungle in stories. The real thing was much darker and deeper. Birdsong and monkey screeches echoed all around them. Strange, rich smells of flowers and bark and animals blasted them from all sides. Crooked branches scraped their fur and grabbed their tails. Soon the leaves were so thick they blocked out the sun. The deeper they went, the darker it got.

It got very, very dark.

"In case you were wondering, there are probably hundreds of different birds and animals watching us right this very minute," Henry said. "Snakes, too. They're very sneaky."

Sometimes Wally wished Henry didn't know quite so much.

Puggly stood taller and walked with her tail held high. She *loved* to be noticed. Wally, however, crept low to the ground.

Wally felt something ooze across his paw. He

yanked his paw up and shook the thing away. It was just a damp leaf. A moment later, he was sure a snake was crawling up his hind leg. But it was only a vine.

Giggling, Piggly wrapped her legs around the vine and swung herself off the ground. "Ahoooooooy!" she barked, whipping through the trees.

Puggly aimed her bamboo berry shooter at her sister as she swung by. *"Ptooey!"* she spat, blowing berries at Piggly. "Gotcha!"

Their barks echoed through the jungle. Wally wondered if anyone was listening.

The pugs swung back and forth on the vines until they got bored. "I'm starving!" Piggly whined, plopping back to the ground.

"And I'm ready to find the treasure," said Puggly. "I hope it's a box full of sparkly stuff. With a crown fit for a queen like me!"

Suddenly, Henry stopped. "Listen," he said.

The three dogs all parked on their haunches
and did as they were told. "I don't hear anything," murmured Wally.

"It's quiet," said Henry. "Too quiet." He
studied the map. He marked their place with

his finger. "If we were on the right track, we would hear the rest of the crew barking. What if we lost the trail?"

Wally and the pugs sniffed at the ground, trying to pick up their friends' scent. Wally thought he caught a whiff of Steak-Eye, who always smelled like stew.

He snuffled in the dirt, trying to sniff out the captain or Curly. But instead, he discovered a trace of someone he didn't recognize.

There was someone else nearby. Or some-*thing.*

He looked up to ask the pugs if they smelled it, too. And that's when he saw it: a pair of eyes, hiding in the darkness. Something was watching them. Something big! Wally pressed his body against Henry's legs to urge his friend to move. Then he barked to signal danger to the pugs.

Henry frowned into the darkness. Piggly and Puggly growled. Wally shivered.

The creature's eyes glowed in the dark.

That's when all four brave pirates had the same idea at the same time: *run!*

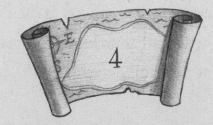

A Beastly Buzz

The four friends charged through the woods. They leaped over stumps and ducked under branches. They scrambled between bushes and wiggled over wet leaves and twisty vines. Wally wasn't sure where they were running to, and he wasn't sure what they were running away from. But he was sure it was something awful. And he was sure he was going to keep running until he couldn't run anymore.

Finally, when his lungs felt as if they might burst, Wally slowed and then stopped. The pugs were out of breath, too. Their tongues hung from their mouths like fat pieces of ham. Henry bent over to catch his breath and take a swig of water from his canteen.

"Did you see it?" Wally asked Piggly. "Did you see what was watching us?"

Piggly arfed. "Aye. It was a great and terrible beastie."

"A monster," Puggly panted. "Must be after the treasure."

"A monster?" Wally asked, wide-eyed. "What kind of monster?"

"Well, I didn't *exactly* see the thing," Piggly said. "But I know it was huge."

"Be glad it didn't catch us," Puggly agreed.

Wally was very glad. He was also very tired. He turned in a circle and lay down, panting.

Maybe he could sneak in a little nap. As soon as he closed his eyes, he heard it.

Buzz . . . Buzz . . . He opened one eye and saw the pugs batting around a papery grayish-brown ball. Except the ball was buzzing.

"Arr-*ooooo!*" Wally woofed. He knew that sound. That was the sound of angry bees. Piggly and Puggly were playing with a beehive!

A moment later, the bees swarmed. Wally felt a sharp sting on his nose. "Ouch!" he cried, swatting at his nose with a paw.

"In case you were wondering," Henry said, "there's more where that came from. We better get out of here fast!"

The group ran faster than ever, trying to escape the swarm of angry bees. Puggly's beads and ribbons kept catching on things in the jungle. More than once, Wally and Henry had to turn back to help untangle her. Piggly's wiggly

belly jiggled. She had a hard time keeping up.
Finally, Henry tugged Piggly into his arms and
carried her.

Just as Wally started to feel like he couldn't
run any farther, they reached the edge of a river.
Perfect! Wally thought. He was pretty sure bees

couldn't swim. He splashed straight into the water. Henry followed. The pugs buried themselves in some mud on the riverbank.

The cool water was just shallow enough for Wally to stand with his head out of the water. Which was a lucky thing, because Wally didn't know how to swim.

Henry crouched low beside Wally. He held the map high in his hand, safe and dry above the water. "In case you were wondering, we lost the bees, mate."

They were no closer to finding the rest of the crew. But at least they were safe from stings. That was something to celebrate.

Wally splashed around, lapping eagerly at the water. Piggly and Puggly giggled as they played in the mud. They almost forgot about the bees and the treasure hunt and the—

"Beastie!" barked Wally, suddenly remembering. He could hear something crashing through the trees. There was no time to run.

Seconds later, the leaves parted. A black-and-white blur sped toward them at full speed, then stopped just before it hit the water. The creature's eyes glowed bright, the same way they had in the bushes. But now a long speckled nose, two floppy ears, and a panting tongue surrounded the glowing eyes. The monster they'd been running from was nothing more than a spotted Dalmatian puppy, no bigger than Wally.

"Greetings!" the spotted pup said, jumping into the water beside Wally. She swam around, then hopped out onto shore and shook herself off. "Thanks for that grand chase. And welcome to my island! Will you be staying long?"

Growlin' Grace's Adventures

Piggly and Puggly backed into the bushes. As lifelong pirates, they had been taught never to trust anything or anyone right away.

But Wally and Henry—who were still learning the pirate ropes—were friendlier. "Ahoy," said Wally, wagging his tail. "Do you live here?"

"Certainly," said the pup. There was a small black spot around one of her eyes that made it look like she was wearing an eye patch. "I've lived here all my life. The other dogs call me Rosie

because of the pink spot on my nose." Rosie sniffed the air to show them her partly pink patch.

"I'm Wally. This is my best mate, Henry. And we're—"

"In case you were wondering," Henry interrupted, "we're searching for Growlin' Grace's greatest treasure."

"Of course," said Rosie. "Many pirates come

to our island searching for treasure. But none have ever found it."

"Do you know where it is?" Wally asked. A personal tour guide would be much more help-ful than an old treasure map, any day!

Rosie laughed. "It's my job to protect the treasure, silly pup. Not lead people to it."

Wally's eyes widened. "So you're like a guard dog for Growlin' Grace?"

"Treasure Keeper." Rosie sat tall and proud. "Do you know the story of how Growlin' Grace's treasure came to live on this island?"

"No," said Wally. He lay down on the river-bank and waited for Rosie to tell the tale. Wally loved stories. "Piggly! Puggly! Do you want to hear a story?"

The two pugs poked their short snouts out of the bushes and eyed Rosie. Rosie let the little dogs approach her and sniff. After a couple of good long snorts, the pugs were satisfied that the danger had passed. They settled in on the cool grass of the riverbank and panted.

Rosie lowered her voice and began. "Many years ago, when the great salt waters were filled with giant beasts and terrible monsters, there lived a puppy pirate captain more brave and daring than any who had come before her. She and her crew were bold explorers who loved adventures. They sailed across the world, meeting many enemies and discovering new lands and waters along the way. Some people say Growlin' Grace had a touch of magic in her."

Piggly squirmed forward and asked, "Why?"

Rosie smiled. "Because everywhere Grace went, she found treasure."

"Jewels?" Puggly wondered.

"Gold?" said Wally.

Rosie cocked her head to one side. "No one

knows for sure. But Growlin' Grace became famous for her treasure-hunting skills. Every pirate from all corners of the world wanted to join her crew, so they could have a chance to be a part of Grace's explorations and discoveries. They say the adventures her crew had were the greatest in all the world. But one day . . ." Rosie stopped to lap up some water in the river.

Henry, who had been relaxing on his back on the bank, opened one eye and smiled at Rosie sleepily.

"One day what?" asked Wally. "What happened?"

"One day, her ship set off in search of the legendary Sea Slug. It was a beast so terrible no ship could pass it without being slimed or gobbled up. Before they set sail, Growlin' Grace decided she should leave her most precious treasure somewhere for safekeeping. So she came to the Boneyard. She buried her treasure here and surrounded it with the watchful eyes of my pack. She made just one map that would help her find the booty when she finally came back for it."

"Did they find the Sea Slug?" Wally whispered. "What happened then?"

Rosie's eyes sparkled. "Well . . ."

Piggly and Puggly snorted and spun in circles, eager to hear the rest of the story.

"Growlin' Grace and her crew sailed into the deepest, darkest uncharted waters . . . and were never heard from again."

Wally gasped. "Never again? She never came back for her treasure?"

"No one knows what happened to them," said Rosie. "Some pups are certain that Grace knew she would never be back. Many believe she left her treasure here with the hopes that

someday another worthy puppy pirate might find it. But no one has. And now her treasure map is long lost."

Wally leaped to his feet. He yipped, "No it's not! We have the map!"

Piggly and Puggly tried to shush him, but it was too late. Suddenly, dozens more spotted pups appeared at the edges of the trees. Rosie's tail straightened in warning. Her smile was gone when she said, "I hope you don't think you'll be taking that treasure. Many unworthy pups have tried before, but none have succeeded. As Treasure Keepers, it's our job to make sure it stays that way."

Trapped!

"What makes you think we be unworthy?" barked Piggly.

"What's *unworthy*?" whispered Wally.

Puggly said, "She's tryin' to say we don't deserve to find that treasure." Then she growled and blew berries through the bamboo straw, warning the other dogs to get back. "Yo ho haroo! We're gonna find that treasure, and there's nothing you can do to stop us."

Rosie bared her teeth. "Oh, we don't need to stop you. The booby traps will do that job for us."

"Booby traps?" Wally asked nervously.

Rosie chuckled, but there was nothing friendly about it. "This island is full of them," she said. "Growlin' Grace didn't want just anyone finding her treasure. So we made sure our traps would catch any unworthy pirates trying to get their paws on her booty. In fact, they've already caught the rest of your crew."

Wally yipped in alarm. "What do you mean?"

"See for yourself," Rosie said, cocking her head in the direction of the dark jungle.

"Come on!" Piggly said, charging off into the trees.

Puggly followed close behind. "We have to save our crew!" she barked.

Rosie glared at Wally and warned him, "The pack and I will be watching. I would wish you luck . . . but luck won't help you now." Without another word, she and her pack slipped back into the bushes and disappeared.

Wally and Henry raced into the jungle after the pugs. The four friends climbed over tree roots. They charged through the thick, damp vines. But everyone stopped when a familiar bark rang out ahead.

"Avast! That sounds like Curly!" shouted Wally. He took off toward the barking.

When Wally ran as fast as his fluffy legs would carry him, it was impossible for the pugs or Henry to match his pace. So Wally was the first to see what Curly was barking about . . . and it wasn't good.

The whole crew was trapped inside a giant net. The trap was hanging from a tall branch,

spinning round and round and round!

"Wally! You're alive!" yipped Curly as soon as she saw Wally flying toward her. She was the only puppy pirate who was not stuck in the net. "I'm so glad you found us. I can't get these scurvy dogs out of that trap on me own."

"What happened?" panted Wally.

Curly quickly said, "Well, we were following the captain through the forest, lookin' for the treasure. We made it this far across the island before Captain Red Beard told us he forgot the map on the ship. That's when we realized we had lost the four of you, too."

Piggly waddled into the clearing and collapsed in a heap at Curly's feet. Puggly rolled on top of her sister and snorted. Henry came last and announced, "Looks like you all are in a whole lot of trouble."

Curly sniffed. "We stopped to come up with a plan, and the captain was feelin' hungry. When he saw a big, meaty pile of bones, he pounced. But the bones were bait for a booby trap! We all got scooped up into the net." She boasted, "I'm tiny, so I was able to wriggle out. But the others are stuck, and I can't get 'em out on me own."

The net spun slowly, fifteen feet in the air. Inside, the crew was a tangle of snouts and paws.

"Ow! Watch yourself!" yelped Old Salt when Red Beard's tail thwacked him in the head.

The ship's cranky cook, Steak-Eye, howled, "Arrrrr-*ooooo*! Ya scurvy dog, you're squeezin' me into jelly." The tiny cook was squished between an enormous Great Dane and the captain, right in the middle of the pile of puppies.

Piggly giggled. "Look at Steak-Eye! His eyes might pop outta his head."

Puggly snorted. "His eyes *always* look like that. He's a Chihuahua."

Captain Red Beard rolled and spun again. "Why's it so crowded in this hammock? This might be the worst nap I've ever taken."

Old Salt groaned. "This is a trap, Captain, remember? Not a hammock. This is not a nap."

"This is a trap?" yelped Red Beard. "Oh, right. A trap." Suddenly, he began to howl, "*Help! Help!* We're trapped."

Curly sighed and looked at the others. "Anyone have an idea how to get them down?"

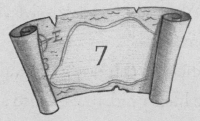

Knot So Fast

Wally, the pug sisters, and Curly discussed the best way to free the rest of the crew. "How 'bout I shoot 'em down?" suggested Puggly. She and Piggly blew berries at their friends, giggling merrily when they splatted against fur.

"Maybe the crew could chew themselves out of the rope?" suggested Wally.

Piggly barked in agreement. "Steak-Eye has super sharp teeth."

Curly thought for a moment. "What we really

need is for someone to untie the knot." She glanced at Henry, then said to Wally, "Your boy has hands. Maybe he can be of some use."

Wally thought this was a great idea, and it seemed like Henry did, too. He had already begun to climb a nearby tree. "In case you were wondering," Henry announced, "this is a simple poacher's knot. Every great pirate knows knots! All I need to do is untie it."

As Henry worked, Wally rushed to the edge of the clearing and gathered palm fronds in his mouth. He piled them under the trap. When his mates fell from the tree, he wanted to make sure they had something soft to land on.

Henry used the hard edges of the magnet to loosen the tricky parts of the knot that his fingers couldn't grasp. The trapped puppy pirates yelped as the trap began to swing to and fro. With each one of Henry's tugs, the pouch full of dogs swayed faster and faster.

"My tummy feels worse than when Steak-Eye makes mystery meat hash," one dog moaned.

The knot began to slip. Then—

Snap!

The net broke open. The crew of puppy pirates rained down onto the leafy jungle floor. The dogs yelped and squealed when they

landed, but no one seemed badly hurt.

Wally ran over to check on Old Salt. The old dog was licking a scrape on his paw, but otherwise seemed fine. "Are you okay, Old Salt?" asked Wally.

Old Salt muttered, "Don't be worryin' about me. I've survived much worse things than a little fall from a tree."

After the crew had all licked their wounds, Wally told the others about meeting Rosie and her pack.

Captain Red Beard said, "Treasure Keepers, eh? And they said there are more traps? Ah, I do love a good booby trap. When ya find a trap, it means you're on the right track! It means there's somethin' ahead that's worth protecting."

"We may well be on the right track," snipped Curly, "but without the map, we're no closer to finding the treasure now than we were a year ago."

"We have the map," announced Wally. "Henry remembered to bring it along when we left the ship."

Curly looked surprised. "Your boy? The human? *He* has the map?"

"Yep," said Wally proudly. He nudged the map out of his friend's pocket with his nose.

Curly cocked her head at Henry again. "Well, shiver me timbers, the boy's done two things right in one day."

Henry unrolled the map. Then, together, he and Red Beard studied it. "All right, me crew," said Red Beard, taking charge. "Carry on this way! We be looking for an X to mark the spot."

Curly said, "Um, Captain? I don't think there's an actual X by the treasure. Usually, the X just marks the spot on the map."

Red Beard looked confused, then nodded. "Ah, yes. Of course. That's what I meant. Okay. Onward!"

Before they set off, Steak-Eye passed around snacks. Soon, everyone but Piggly—who was *always* hungry—had a full belly and was ready to continue.

Then Curly suggested that each of the dogs find a giant leaf to use as protection from the hot sun. They found a tree with leaves shaped like curved umbrellas. When they were strapped to the puppy pirates' backs with vines, the leaves

helped keep them cool and comfortable in the midday heat.

As they tiptoed over a fraying rope bridge, Red Beard kept them all calm by singing pirate songs about treasure.

While they walked single file along the ridge of a steep mountain, Old Salt helped them focus by telling stories from his many years of pirate adventures.

And when they snuck under a roaring waterfall—protected from the spray by their leafy umbrellas—Piggly and Puggly told jokes to keep everyone smiling. It felt good to have the whole crew back together.

Just past the waterfall, the captain ordered his crew to stop. "Avast!" Up ahead, something shiny glinted in the sunlight. Everyone squinted for a better look. Red Beard's tail began to wag, and he barked, "The booty!"

They all ran. For there it was, right in the open for anyone to see: *a golden treasure chest*!

Henry and Wally whooped with joy as they chased after the others. But when they neared the chest, Wally realized something wasn't right. On the map, the X to mark the spot was in the middle of a big, open space, near the ocean. But this treasure chest was sitting at the top of a huge hill. Here, they were surrounded by trees and rocks and the waterfall.

"Don't act without thinking," Old Salt warned them. "Too many pups lose their heads at the sight of treasure."

But the captain was already nosing open the lid of the treasure box. When it popped open, a horrible smell came rushing out at the crew. It was worse than rotten apples and spoiled meat. The dogs all scrambled backward, but they soon realized that the smell was the least of their problems.

Something rumbled, and the ground began to shake. Rocks danced around them as the earth tilted like their ship did in a terrible storm. The sand and dirt under their feet slipped away, taking Red Beard and his crew along for a ride.

"It's a mudslide!" woofed the captain. "What do we do?"

Thinking quickly, Piggly and Puggly came up with an idea.

"Everyone untie your shade leaf!" Piggly

said. "You can use it as a surfboard to surf the mud."

"Like this!" Puggly cried, leaping onto her leaf and riding a wave of mud all the way to the bottom of the hill.

Piggly threw herself down after her sister, howling with glee. "Yo ho haroooo!"

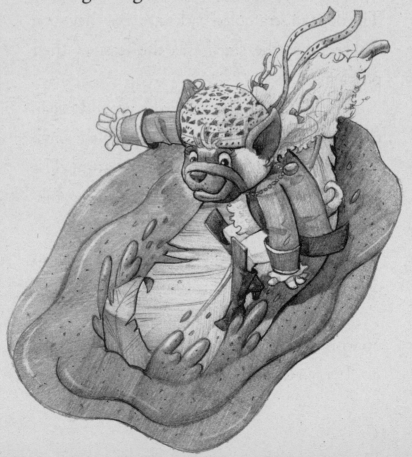

The other dogs leaped onto their leaves and followed them down.

"Aye, aye!" barked Red Beard. "I'm surfin'!"

Right at the bottom of the hill, next to a gorgeous sand beach, was the biggest mudhole any of them had ever seen. *Splat!* The sticky mud felt cold and refreshing after a long day of treasure hunting.

Puggly barked, "This is pug-glorious!"

Wally agreed. He wished *all* booby traps were this fun. He and the other pups wrestled and rolled and dug holes in the mud for a few moments before they heard Old Salt's warning bark.

The ground rumbled again. "It's another trap!" Wally yelped. "Quick, we have to get out of here!" But it was too late. No one was going anywhere.

A Little Riddle

Dozens of wooden poles sprouted out of the dirt. They stretched up, up, up toward the clouds. The puppy pirate crew scrambled to get out of the mud, but the gooey ground made it impossible for them to move quickly enough.

The poles were too close together to squeeze through. Too sturdy to push over. Too thick to chew through.

There was no way out.

"Sticks!" howled Captain Red Beard joyfully. "Lots of sticks for us to chew!"

"Not sticks," mumbled Old Salt. "This is a cage. We're trapped."

Wally paced the edges of the cage. He noticed something strange. Each bar had a number carved into it. The numbers went in order, from 1 to 317. A cage with more than *three hundred*

bars? Wally sighed. It was hopeless. Even Curly couldn't escape this trap.

Henry pulled out the map. "I don't see a cage on this map anywhere, so this must be another booby trap to guard the treasure."

"Thank you, Captain Obvious," grumbled Curly.

Wally tugged at the first mate's tail, warning her to leave his friend alone.

"Look!" sniffed Piggly. She, too, had been sniffing around the edges of the large cage, searching for hidden food. Instead, she found strange words carved into one of the bars:

IF YE BE WORTHY, THEN YE SHALL
KNOW . . . THAT THREE BY THREE IS
HOW YE SHALL GO.

"I wonder if it could be a clue?" asked Wally. "There are numbers in the riddle and numbers carved into the poles. That must mean *something*."

"I bet these words are a clue!" agreed Henry.

"Three and three . . . ," muttered Red Beard. "I've got . . . let's see . . . one, two, three paws. Three paws!"

"Four paws," corrected Old Salt with a sigh. "I've got three paws."

Red Beard went on. "Dogs have one nose. Two eyes. Three what?"

"Hmm, three by three . . . ," said Curly. "What if it's simple math? Three plus three is

six. What happens if we press the pole with a six carved into it?"

Piggly launched herself at the bar labeled with the number six. As soon as she hit it, it swung open and she found herself on the other side of the cage. "Ahoy in there!" she snorted at her friends.

Puggly tried next, but this time, the sixth bar wouldn't budge. She barked in confusion. "What now?"

The puppies didn't get it. They had solved the riddle. So why did it only work once? And how were the rest of them supposed to get out?

"Three by three," Wally murmured, knocking ideas around in his head. Suddenly, he came up with a new one. "What if we have to go *another* three?" he said.

"Keep up, Walty," the captain snapped. "We can't *go* anywhere. That's the problem."

"No, what if we *count* another three?" Wally

asked. "We started with the sixth bar. What's three past that?"

Puggly counted it out with her paws. "Seven . . . eight . . . nine!" She flung herself at the ninth bar—and sailed right through.

"In case you were wondering, I think we need to count by threes until we're all out of here!" Henry said.

Old Salt went next, counting three more bars to number twelve, and pushing through to freedom. Then Steak-Eye (fifteen), then Wally (eighteen), then the rest of the crew. Like a good captain, Red Beard took up the rear— but Wally had to tell him which bar to press. Hard as he tried, Red Beard couldn't seem to count by threes.

On the other side of the cage, tall palm trees grew out of the sand. Wally thought they looked like little rockets exploding high above the beach.

When Henry took out the treasure map to check their location, Wally noticed that Rosie and the pack of Dalmatians were back. They were waiting right along the water's edge. Wally had a feeling that that meant the treasure was close by.

Wally introduced the captain and his crew to the Treasure Keepers.

Rosie growled, "Somehow, you escaped the net trap. Then you found a way to *enjoy* the mudslide. You have solved Growlin' Grace's riddle. I will admit that your band of pirates has gotten much closer to the treasure than any others who have come before you." The Dalmatian stood tall. "The map has taken you this far, but now you're on your own."

Red Beard gazed around with his sharp terrier eyes. "On the map, there's an X by a tree. So there must be treasure under one of these trees."

Wally thought that sounded right. There was just one problem: *Which tree?* He started sniffing around in the sand. If he couldn't see the treasure, maybe he could *smell* it.

"We're dogs," Curly reminded her crew. "We were built to dig. We know the treasure's under here somewhere. So I say we dig!"

The puppy pirates took off. Sand and paws flew everywhere. Rosie and the Treasure Keepers watched carefully. As the afternoon stretched on, they began to smile. Not one of the puppy pirates had any luck. Soon the entire beach was filled with holes—but there was still no sign of treasure.

Wally stopped for a break. He was hot, sandy, and thirsty. Around him, he could see that the rest of the crew was growing tired, too. Piggly had settled in under a tree, where she was trying to knock open a coconut with her magnet. Puggly was grooming herself, trying to clean the mud off her ribbons. Henry, who had no paws, was still struggling to dig his first hole.

What if this doesn't work? Wally wondered. What if they *never* found Growlin' Grace's treasure? He knew they must be missing an important clue. Growlin' Grace wanted to make her treasure hard to find. But she wouldn't have made it *impossible*. He stared up into the vast blue sky, watching the trees flutter in the ocean air. And that's when he saw it—an X! Not an X on the ground, but an X made of trees.

Two palm trees tilted out of the sand. Their trunks crossed each other. Reaching high into the air, side by side, they looked very much like an X.

What a clever way to mark the spot!

Wally leaped up and began to bark. "The trees!" he yipped. "The X is *in* the trees!"

Trick Sand

The puppy pirates all gathered under the giant X. They let Captain Red Beard dig first. He picked a spot right between the two trees and pawed at the wet sand.

"Arrrr!" growled Red Beard. "Look out, treasure, here I come!"

Then he began to sink.

Down, down, down.

"It's quicksand!" yowled Curly.

"Quicksand? You're kiddin' me." Red Beard's four paws were sinking quickly in the oozing muck.

Four dogs on the crew stepped forward to help save their captain. One pulled at Red Beard's ear with his teeth. Another snapped the captain's beard in her mouth and tugged. A third got a mouthful of the scruff at the back of Red Beard's neck. Finally, the big Great Dane

got his nose up under the captain's belly and lifted. Working together, they dragged Red Beard to safety.

Growlin' Grace's treasure was down at the bottom of that quicksand. The puppy pirates were sure of it. They were close enough that they could almost *smell* it! But what good did it do? They couldn't dig without sinking. And if they couldn't dig, how could they get their paws on the treasure?

"We've got ourselves a little sit-you-station," said Red Beard, rubbing his paws in dry sand to clean off the quicksand.

"I think you mean *situation*, Captain?" offered Piggly.

"As I said," growled Red Beard. "This is a situation with no pollution."

"*Solution?*" wondered Curly.

"Exactly!" agreed Red Beard. "So what is it?"

"The solution?" said Curly. "Well, the only solution I can think of is for one brave and mighty pirate to take the plunge. One of us has to get down there."

"I already did that," said Red Beard. "It made my toes feel funny."

"I've got an idea." A shaggy Old English sheepdog giggled. "Let's dangle one of the pugs from a leash and drop 'em in. We've got two on our crew, so we can afford to lose one, eh?"

Piggly and Puggly growled and snapped at the sheepdog.

Curly stood as tall as a tiny poodle could get. "I'll go in. I'm small and light, and I can hold my breath longer than any other dog on the crew. If you tie a rope around me, you should be able to pull me out once I have the treasure."

"No," Wally yelped. "It's too risky!" Being on the crew meant looking out for his fellow pirates.

He couldn't let Curly put herself in danger.

"You got a better idea, pup?" Curly asked. "Because otherwise—"

"Wait!" Wally said. "I do have a better idea. It's . . . it's . . ." He thought very hard. Then Wally snatched Piggly's magnet out of her paws. He remembered the pugs dangling the magnet through the spy hole that morning, and how they told him it would stick to the metal map box. If the treasure chest had metal on it, maybe the magnet could pull it to the surface. "We can use this!"

Captain Red Beard was impressed. "It's worth a shot."

Using his expert knot skills, Henry tied the magnet to the end of Piggly's bamboo shooter with vines. It was like a fishing rod—with a giant magnet dangling from the end.

Captain Red Beard held the rod as the crew

lowered the rope into the quicksand. At first, the magnet just sat like a lump on the top of the sand. But after a few moments, it began to sink into the pit. Slowly at first, then faster. The line stretched and pulled. The pups held their breath as they waited for it to hit something. The magnet just kept sinking—deeper and deeper and deeper.

Red Beard worked with the strongest pups on the crew to hold the pole tight. But it seemed that the sand was stronger. Before long, the line grew tight. And the sand began to tug the dogs toward the quicksand.

They had almost run out of rope. If the magnet didn't hit the chest soon, this treasure hunt would be a bust.

Snap!

Everyone felt it when the magnet snapped on to something deep in the ground. When the team of pups pulled on the rope with their teeth, they felt sure *something* was on their line. They pulled and pulled and pulled and pulled and—

Pop! The treasure chest came flying out of the quicksand. The crew dragged it onto solid ground. Everyone gathered around, even Rosie and her pack.

"Oh, my!" gasped Rosie. "It's Growlin' Grace's treasure chest. You found it!"

Even though the chest was coated in gooey sand, it was easy to see the huge jewels gleaming on the top of chest. Puggly squealed, eager to pop it open. "Jewels! Jewels! Jewels!" she said, bubbling with excitement.

Captain Red Beard urged everyone to step back. "Give the treasure room to breathe," he said. Then he eased open the latch and flipped the lid. The puppies rushed forward again. No one could wait to see what was inside.

When Wally poked his nose up over the edge of the chest, his hopes—and everyone else's—came crashing down. For inside the chest was . . . a bunch of old maps.

The captain scratched his beard and said what everyone was thinking. "Is that all?"

The Real Treasure

Wally had never seen a real pirate treasure before. But he was pretty sure there was supposed to be a lot more gold.

"I was hoping for at least a few yummy dog treats," muttered Piggly.

"Just maps," said Henry glumly. "This was a whole lot of hassle for a bunch of old maps."

"At least they aren't blank!" Puggly said.

Wally caught Rosie looking at the rest of her pack. She seemed as surprised as everyone else!

Curious, Wally nosed around inside the box. One of the pieces of parchment was different from all the others. It was a letter. Carefully, he pulled it out with his teeth.

"What's this?" asked Henry, taking it gently from Wally's mouth. "Ooh! It's a letter from Growlin' Grace."

To the worthy pirates who have found me bounty:

Congratulations. You have found my greatest treasure.

Bet you thought you'd find gold, eh? Ha!

Sure, I found plenty of riches in me travels. But in all me years as a pirate, I learned that the best treasure any pirate can hope for is the promise of more adventure.

In this box, you will find the maps me crew put together of all our greatest travels. These maps will lead you to the strangest and most wondrous places I've seen in all me days. I'm leaving them for a new group of worthy pirates. I hope you will use them to guide and inspire your own adventures.

Have fun. Make sure you add to me collection with new travels of your own.

Ahoy, mighty pirates!

—Growlin' Grace

When they had finished reading the letter, everyone sat quietly. Finally, Captain Red Beard broke the silence and cheered, "Hip, hip hooray!"

The rest of the crew joined in and cheered, too. More adventures! This *was* the greatest treasure Growlin' Grace could have left them. More than riches or jewels or the yummiest bones in all the world.

Only Puggly looked disappointed. She had really been hoping for a crown.

Wally nudged his friend and said, "Don't be sad, Puggly. Now that we have all these maps, we're sure to find a crown fit for a queen on one of our *next* adventures. Anyway, you're the fanciest pirate on our crew, even without jewels."

That cheered her up. She pranced around the beach.

"Let's get this treasure chest back to the ship," said Red Beard. "Adventure awaits!"

"Wait," said Rosie, stepping forward. "You can't take our treasure!"

"You said you wouldn't stop us from searching for the treasure," Wally reminded Rosie.

"Exactly," Rosie said. "We didn't stop you. And you found it. Now you can go."

"We're not leaving without that treasure!" Red Beard barked.

"And you're not leaving *with* it." Rosie and her pack stepped between the pirate crew and the treasure chest. The two packs stared each other down.

Old Salt coughed and said, "I can see you Dalmatians want to keep the treasure here."

"If you take the treasure," yapped Rosie, "then the Boneyard is just a plain old island! No one will come here to search for treasure anymore. We won't have anything to protect!"

"But I know our captain would like to take

Growlin' Grace's maps to guide our crew's adventures," Old Salt continued.

Red Beard barked, "Finders keepers!"

"I have a solution," Old Salt said calmly. "Rosie, your pack doesn't actually want *this* treasure for yourselves . . . ya just want *some* treasure buried on the island. Is that true?"

Rosie nodded.

Old Salt coughed. "Then I think we owe it to these pups to bury a treasure on this island for another band of pirates to find someday. A great pirate should always leave a little something behind for safekeeping before heading off on the next adventure. Don'tcha think, Cap'n?"

Curly added, "Just think . . . hundreds of pirates could come to this island searching for *your* treasure, Captain Red Beard."

Red Beard's eyes lit up. "The Boneyard will be the hiding place for *Red Beard's* greatest treasure! I like the sound of that!"

Rosie and the other Dalmatians barked their approval.

The only trouble was, no one had any idea what they could bury. They had no gold, or maps, or jewels.

Finally, Wally had an idea. "What if we each bury something that's special to us? Growlin' Grace's greatest treasure was her map collection, because they reminded her of her greatest adventures with her crew." He thought for a moment before he said, "My greatest treasure is my pirate bandanna. Because the day I got this bandanna, I knew I'd finally found my home on the ship with all of you."

"I'm gonna bury my best soup bone," said Steak-Eye, stepping forward to drop his bone into the box.

Puggly stepped forward, too. "And I'm going to bury my favorite necklace. That way, this box will have something *fancy* for the next gal who digs it up."

Piggly shot one last blueberry out of her bamboo shooter and said, "I'll hide this for another lucky prankster to find someday!"

Henry stepped forward and placed a picture he had drawn of him and Wally into the chest. Wally tossed his bandanna on top of it.

One by one, everyone on the crew dropped an item that meant something special to them into the chest. Soon it was filled to the top.

As Red Beard, the pugs, Wally, Henry, and the others lowered the chest back into the pit of quicksand, Rosie said, "Thank you. We promise to keep your greatest treasures safe for many years to come. And we hope you'll be back someday to fetch them."

"We will," promised Wally. "But not for a long time."

After all, now that they had Growlin' Grace's maps, they could go anywhere! Do anything!

As the Dalmatian puppies led the way down the beach, the *Salty Bone* loomed tall and proud in the distance. Wally couldn't wait to get back to the ship and set sail. Their next puppy pirate adventure was waiting!

All paws on deck!

Another Puppy Pirates adventure
is on the horizon.
Here's a sneak peek at

Catnapped!

It was an ambush! The entire kitten pirate crew was crawling over the hillside. The cats were angry, all hisses and claws. The town pups ran off, but the puppy pirates prepared for a fight.

Most of the puppy pirates, anyway. Not Spike. He just roamed in circles, shaking with terror. "What do we do? What do we *do-oooo-ooooo?*"

Captain Red Beard pushed to the front of his crew. He went nose to nose with the kitten captain. "We *had* a deal, Captain Lucinda the Loud! We no attacky you, you no attacky us."

Lucinda the Loud hissed. "We had a deal . . . until your pugs broke the rules. Bad dogs! You should know better than to play catnip pranks on Moopsy and Boopsy."

"Uh-oh," Piggly squeaked. She and Puggly quickly backed away from the face-off. They ducked beneath a leafy bush.

"Moopsy and Boopsy?" Puggly snorted, once they were safely out of sight. She tried to hide her giggles inside her cape. "The Siamese cats are named *Moopsy* and *Boopsy*?" Laughing and sneezing, she poked her sister. "Piggly, come with me. I've got an idea!"

No one but Wally noticed the pugs sneak away. All eyes were on the two pirate captains.

"You're outnumbered!" Lucinda the Loud yelled. "You have no choice but to surrender."

"Never!" Red Beard barked. "Puppy pirates, prepare for battle!"

Excerpt copyright © 2015 by Erin Soderberg Downing and Robin Wasserman. Published in the United States by Random House Children's Books, a division of Penguin Random House LLC.